People in My Community

Nurses

By JoAnn Early Macken

Gareth Stevens Publishing

Please visit our Web site, www.garethstevens.com. For a free color catalog of all our high-quality books, call toll free 1-800-542-2595 or fax 1-877-542-2596.

Library of Congress Cataloging-in-Publication Data

Macken, JoAnn Early, 1953-
Nurses / JoAnn Early Macken.
p. cm. – (People in my community)
Includes index.
ISBN 978-1-4339-3807-8 (pbk.)
ISBN 978-1-4339-3808-5 (6-pack)
ISBN 978-1-4339-3806-1 (library binding) –
1. Nurses–Juvenile literature. 2. Nursing–Juvenile literature. I. Title.
RT61.5.M336 2011
610.73–dc22
2010013208

New edition published 2011 by
Gareth Stevens Publishing
111 East 14th Street, Suite 349
New York, NY 10003

Original edition published 2003 by Weekly Reader® Books
An imprint of Gareth Stevens Publishing

Art direction: Haley Harasymiw, Tammy Gruenwald
Page layout: Daniel Hosek, Katherine A. Goedheer
Editorial direction: Kerri O'Donnell, Diane Laska Swanke

Photo credits: Cover, back cover, p. 1 Brad Wilson/The Image Bank/Getty Images; pp. 5, 13, 17 Shutterstock.com; pp. 7, 11, 15, 19, 21 © Gregg Andersen; p. 9 Joe Raedle/Getty Images.

Printed in the United States of America

CPSIA compliance information: Batch #CS10GS: For further information contact Gareth Stevens, New York, New York at 1-800-542-2595.

Table of Contents

Taking Care of People 4

What Nurses Wear 8

A Nurse's Tools 10

Teaching People 18

Glossary. .22

For More Information. 23

Index 24

Boldface words appear in the glossary.

Taking Care of People

Nurses help take care of people who are hurt or sick. They also help people stay healthy.

Some nurses work in doctors' offices or **hospitals**. Some work in schools. Some nurses go to people's homes.

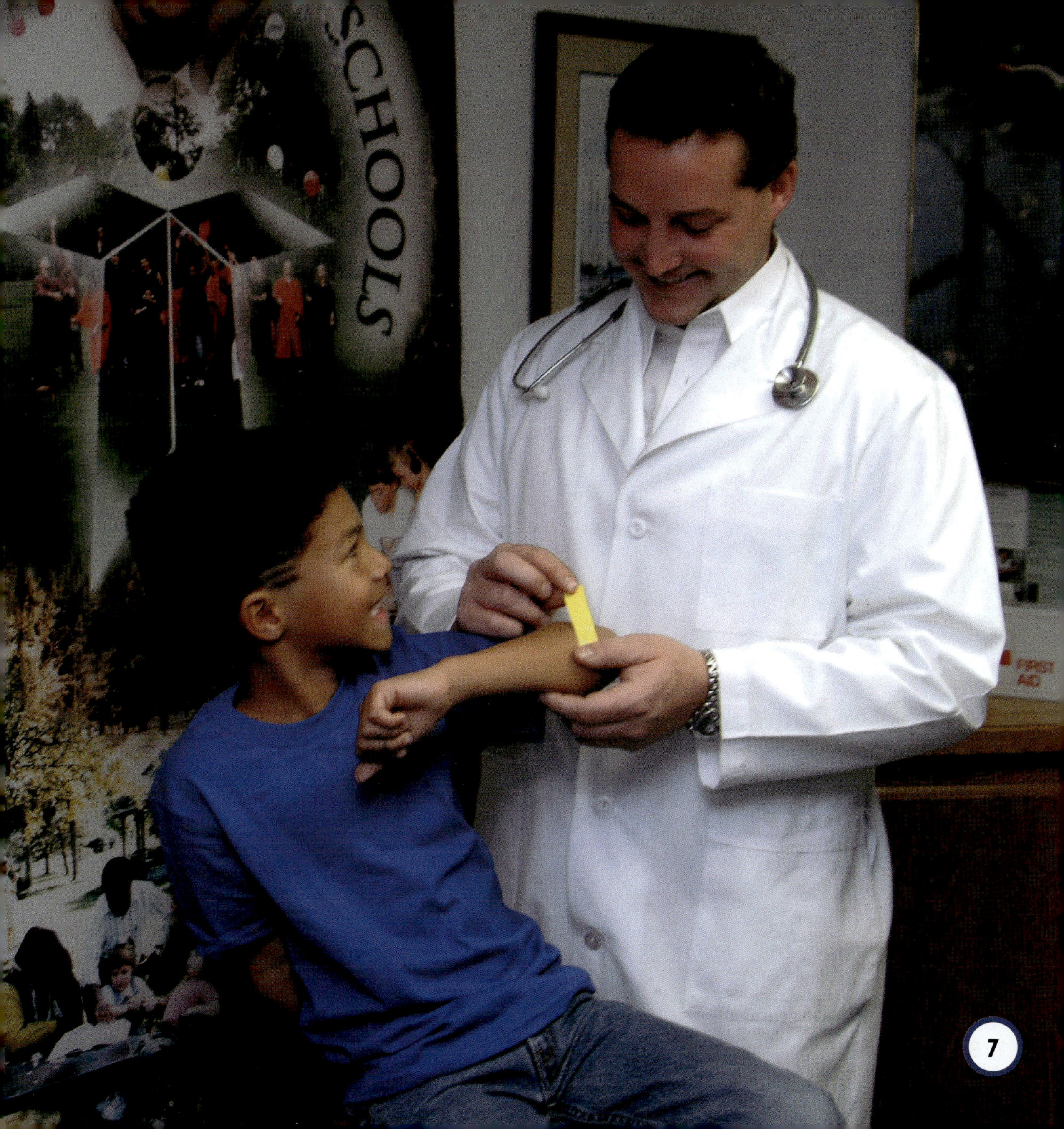
SCHOOLS
FIRST AID

What Nurses Wear

Nurses wear different kinds of clothes. Some wear all white. Some wear colorful shirts. Some wear **scrubs**.

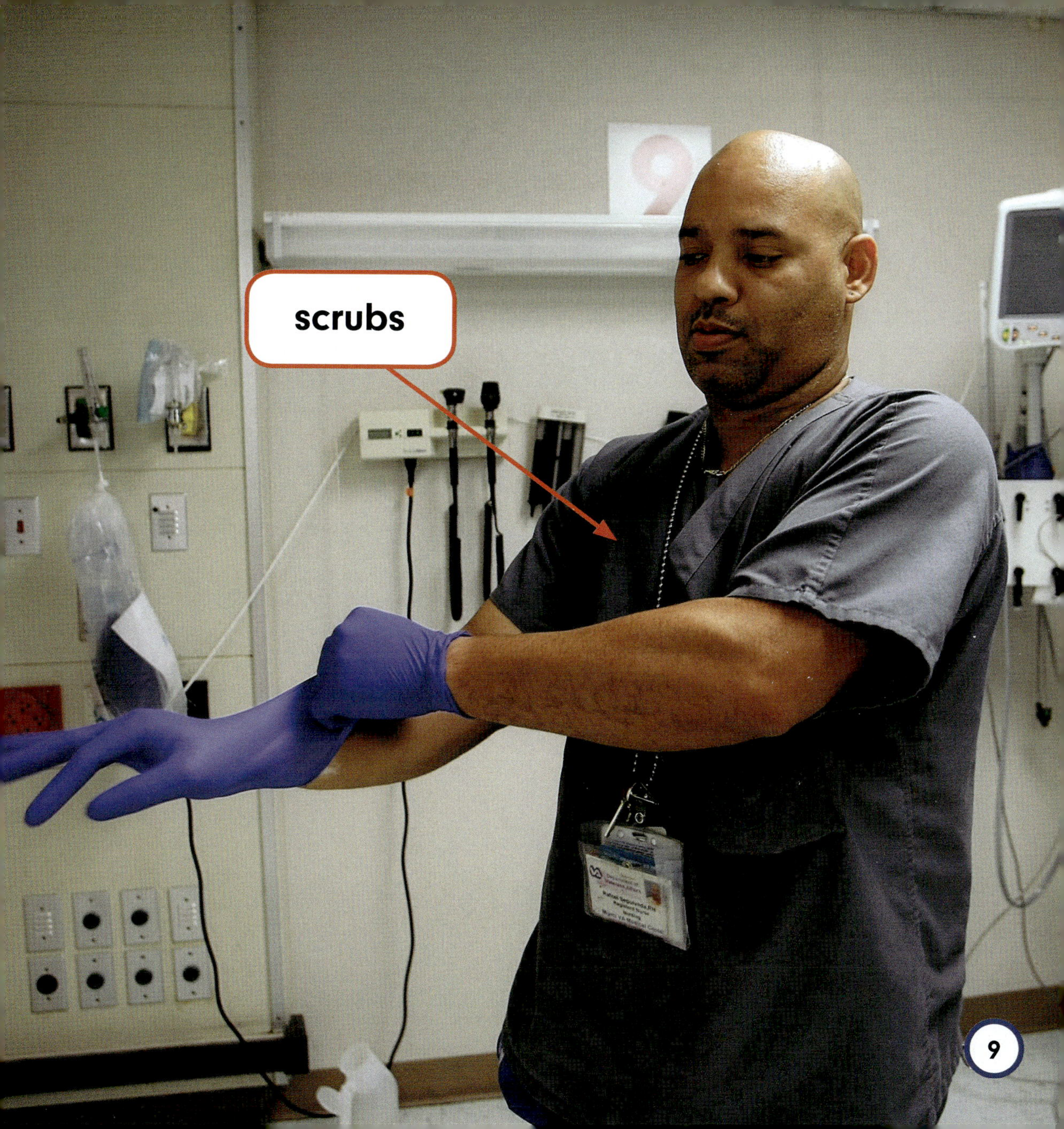
scrubs

A Nurse's Tools

Nurses use a tool called a **thermometer** to check a person's **temperature**. They check a person's heart and breathing with a **stethoscope**.

stethoscope

Nurses use a watch to check a person's heart rate. They use a special cuff to check **blood pressure**.

cuff

Nurses use a **scale** to check your weight. Do you know how much you weigh?

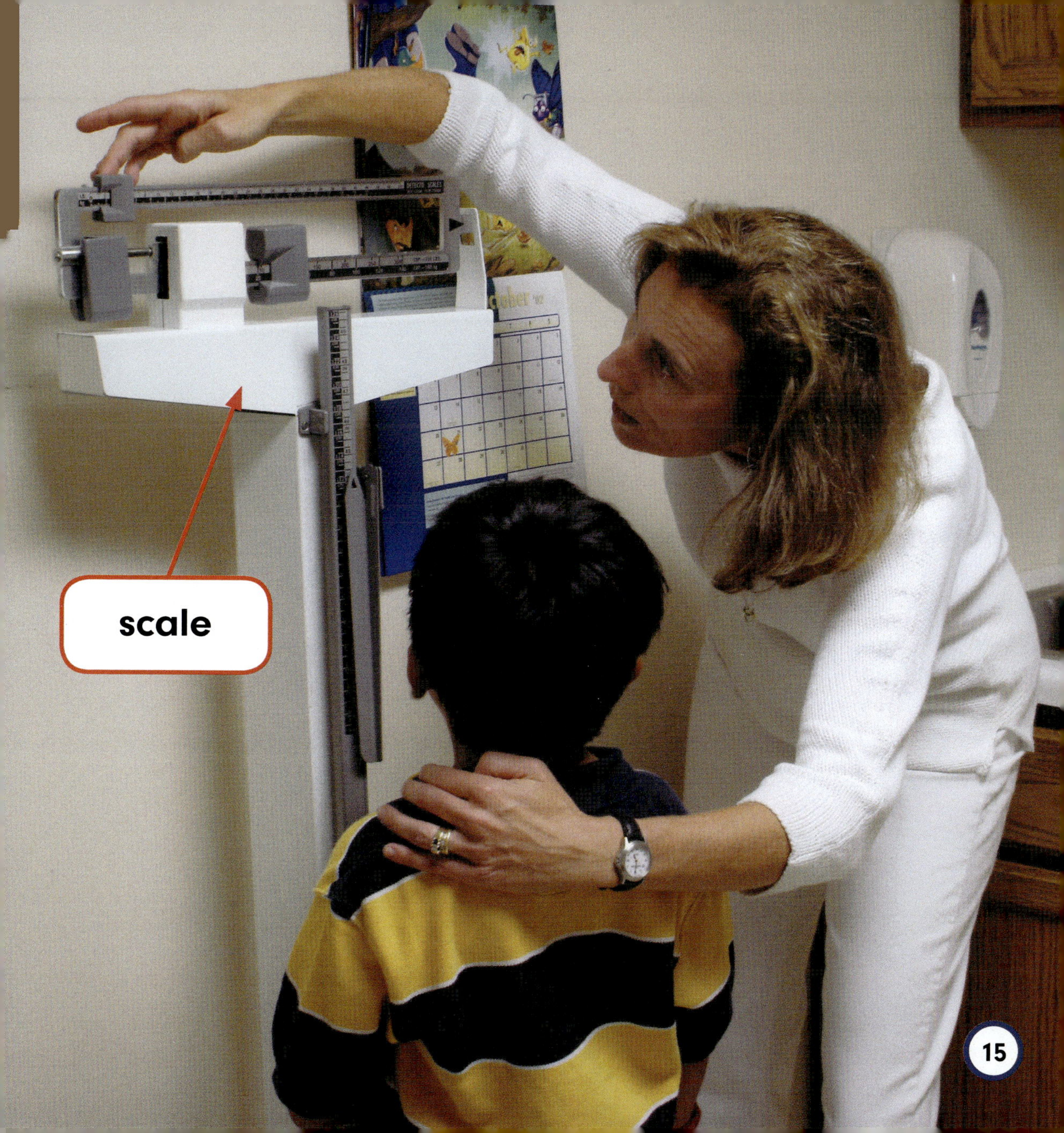
scale

Nurses take notes about people's health. They write their notes on paper or enter them into a computer.

computer

Teaching People

Nurses teach people about staying healthy. They help people learn how to take care of themselves and their families.

Nurses help people. If you are ever hurt or sick, a nurse can help take care of you.

Glossary

blood pressure: the force with which blood moves through our body

hospital: a place that takes care of sick or hurt people

scale: a tool used to measure how heavy something is

scrubs: special clothing worn by a nurse or a doctor

stethoscope: a tool used to hear the heart and listen to breathing

temperature: how hot or cold something is

thermometer: a tool used to measure hot and cold

For More Information

Books

Cunningham, Kevin. *Nurse*. Ann Arbor, MI: Cherry Lake Publishing, 2009.

Kishel, Ann-Marie. *Nurse*. Minneapolis, MN: Lerner Publications, 2007.

Web Sites

Going to the Hospital

kidshealth.org/kid/feel_better/places/hospital.html
Learn about some of the things that happen when you go to the hospital.

Health: Your Body and How It Works

www.brainpop.com/health
Read about keeping healthy. Watch videos about how your body works and what happens if you're sick or hurt.

Publisher's note to educators and parents: Our editors have carefully reviewed these Web sites to ensure that they are suitable for students. Many Web sites change frequently, however, and we cannot guarantee that a site's future contents will continue to meet our high standards of quality and educational value. Be advised that students should be closely supervised whenever they access the Internet.

Index

blood pressure 12
clothes 8
computer 16, 17
cuff 12, 13
doctors' offices 6
healthy 4, 18
hospitals 6
hurt 4, 20
notes 16
people's homes 6
scale 14, 15
schools 6
scrubs 8, 9
sick 4, 20
stethoscope 10, 11
temperature 10
thermometer 10
tools 10
watch 12
weight 14

About the Author

JoAnn Early Macken is the author of children's poetry; two rhyming picture books, *Cats on Judy* and *Sing-Along Songs*; and various other nonfiction series. She teaches children to write poetry and received the Barbara Juster Esbensen 2000 Poetry Teaching Award. JoAnn is a graduate of the MFA in Writing for Children Program at Vermont College. She lives in Wisconsin with her husband and their two sons.